Olga's Song

First published in 2011
by Wayland

Wayland
338 Euston Road
London NW1 3BH

Wayland Australia
Level 17/207 Kent Street
Sydney, NSW 2000

Series Editor: Louise John
Editor: Katie Woolley
Cover design: Paul Cherrill
Design: D.R.ink
Consultant: Shirley Bickler

A CIP catalogue record for this book is available from the British Library.

ISBN 9780750265317

Printed in China

www.hachette.co.uk

Olga's Song

Written by Joe Hackett
Illustrated by Natalie Hinrichsen

WAYLAND

It was the summer holidays and Olga was helping Nana make some cherry jam. She had been staying in the village for two days but already she missed the city and her friends.

"Cheer up, Olga! It's your name day next week," said Nana, as she stirred the jam on the stove. "Everyone called Olga in all of Bulgaria will be celebrating."

"I know, Nana," said Olga grumpily.

Olga was trying to listen to her music player and she didn't want to talk.

"I can teach you a song to sing on your name day," said Nana.

"I hate singing in front of people," moaned Olga.

"Nonsense, I used to sing this song on my name day," said Nana. "It's about a boy and a girl who meet and fall in love at the village well."

Nana closed her eyes and began to sing.

“Nana, I don’t want to sing about a boy!” Olga cried.

“It’s only a song, Olga,” Nana smiled.

Olga didn't want to upset Nana so she began to sing the words.

"You'll have to practise hard all this week," said Nana.

But Olga didn't practise at all. Instead, she sat out in the fields, listening to her music player.

When no one was looking, except for the animals, Olga liked to dance along to the music.

Soon it was Olga's name day and the house was full of aunts and uncles, cousins and friends.

"Go and collect your mum and dad from the bus stop, Olga," said Nana, as she took a loaf of bread out of the oven.

So Olga set off towards the village square. The bus was just arriving and Olga ran to meet her parents.

"We can't wait to hear you sing," said Dad, as they walked back to Nana's house.

"Yes, Nana has told us all about it. She's very excited about you singing," smiled Mum, as she hugged Olga.

Olga gave her a little smile and began to wish she had practised a bit more. She hoped she could remember the words!

That afternoon, after a large lunch, Olga sang the song to her friends and family.

She was a bit nervous, but soon her voice grew stronger. At the end, everyone clapped and cheered.

“That was wonderful, Olga,” cried Nana, giving her a big kiss.

Olga realised she was having fun but, all too soon, it was time for Mum and Dad to go back to the city.

Over the next few days the weather grew hotter and hotter. One day, the village ran out of water completely.

"It's called a drought," said Nana, as she tried to turn on the kitchen tap. "Don't worry. The village well never runs dry."

So Olga and Nana set off to collect water from the well.

Olga lowered a large bucket on a rope down into the well. It landed with a splash!

"You're right, Nana, there is water!" cried Olga, and she quickly pulled the bucket up.

Back home, Nana dipped a glass into the bucket and gave it to Olga.

"Here, taste it," said Nana. "It's the best water in Bulgaria!"

The next day Olga went to collect some more water. As she walked up the hill, she saw a boy at the well.

"Hello. I'm Stefan," he said, as Olga walked towards him. "Who are you?"

"I'm Olga," she said. "I'm staying with my nana for the school holidays."

Suddenly Olga thought about the song. The boy and girl fell in love when they met at a well!

Olga didn't want to fall in love with Stefan! She dropped her empty bucket and ran back home as quickly as she could.

At home Olga told Nana what had happened.

"Don't be silly, little one," Nana laughed, giving Olga a big hug. "I think Stefan just wants to be your friend. There'll be plenty of time to fall in love when you are older!"

The next day Olga went back to the well. Stefan was there, too.

Bravely, she asked him if he wanted to listen to her music player.

"Yes, please!" said Stefan, excitedly.

And, just like that, Olga and Stefan became friends. Nana was right after all!

START READING is a series of highly enjoyable books for beginner readers. **The books have been carefully graded to match the Book Bands widely used in schools.** This enables readers to be sure they choose books that match their own reading ability.

Look out for the Band colour on the book in our Start Reading logo.

The Bands are:

START READING books can be read independently or shared with an adult. They promote the enjoyment of reading through satisfying stories, plays and non-fiction narratives, which are supported by fun illustrations and photographs.

Joe Hackett often visits a village in Bulgaria – one of his favourite countries –because the people are friendly and there's a lot of wildlife to see. He hasn't yet spotted a wolf but he knows they are up there in the forests and mountains somewhere!

Natalie Hinrichsen works in her loft studio in a suburb of Cape Town, South Africa. She has been illustrating children's books since 1996 and in 2005 she won the Vivian Wilkes award for illustration.